Phil May

Phil May's ABC

52 original designs forming 2 humorous alphabets from A to Z

Phil May

Phil May's ABC

52 original designs forming 2 humorous alphabets from A to Z

ISBN/EAN: 9783741193194

Manufactured in Europe, USA, Canada, Australia, Japa

Cover: Foto ©Andreas Hilbeck / pixelio.de

Manufactured and distributed by brebook publishing software
(www.brebook.com)

Phil May

Phil May's ABC

Sunshine and Rain !

PHIL MAY'S ABC

FIFTY·TWO

ORIGINAL DESIGNS

forming

TWO HUMOROUS ALPHABETS

from

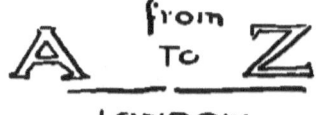

A To Z

LONDON

THE LEADENHALL PRESS LIMITED.

Each initial has been separately Copyrighted.

THE ALPHABETS ARE PRECEDED

LIST OF SUBJECTS.

The subject of collecting prints that may be common to-day and rare to-morrow is one which in these days enters very considerably into the regions of practical and domestic politics. On the principle that nobody keeps what everybody else has, so an etching or a print, which is published by its thousands, often becomes extremely rare in a very short space of time. Many of them are well worth the keeping, well worth the framing, and well worth the hanging. There is a wealth of drawing worth framing from the pens of such men as Phil May ° ‘ ° Too much good work is just now allowed to waste.—*The Sketch.*

See Frontispiece.

Critics.

" Yah, Yah ! "

Mortal Enemies.

Sea-sprites.

Aristocrats.

Distinction.

Famine and Plenty.

The Broken Heart.

The Queen's Recruits.

Tea and Scandal.

"The Jolly Angler."

Halves !

Hide and Seek. Phil MAY.

Orpheus with his Lute.

Getting Money for Father.

Getting Father Home,

Training for the
Circus.

Flowers and Feathers.

A Pair of High Steppers.

"Lost yer Wages—'ole in yer Pocket, eh?"

" "Seated one day on the Organ—"

Hope and Fear.

A Study in Black and White.

Under Compulsion.

To the Rescue!

A Mother's Jealousy

A Long Pull.

Love's Young Dream.

Nabbed.

Set to Partners.

"I see Yer!"

That Little Vulgar Boy.

The Envy of the Court.

"Kish yer Father, Ducky."

"Only a Λ'penny."

Up to Date.

Business.

"Lor! I thought 'e were Alive!"

Cupboard Love.

Penniless.

Won't she Catch it!

To Brighton and Back, 3/6.

Beatitude.

"Don't be sitch a Silly Fool."

All Sorts and Conditions.

Chaffing and Chaffering.

"Carry it, Sir?"

"Hextra, Sir?"

"Come on, Do!"

An Accident.

See Frontispiece.

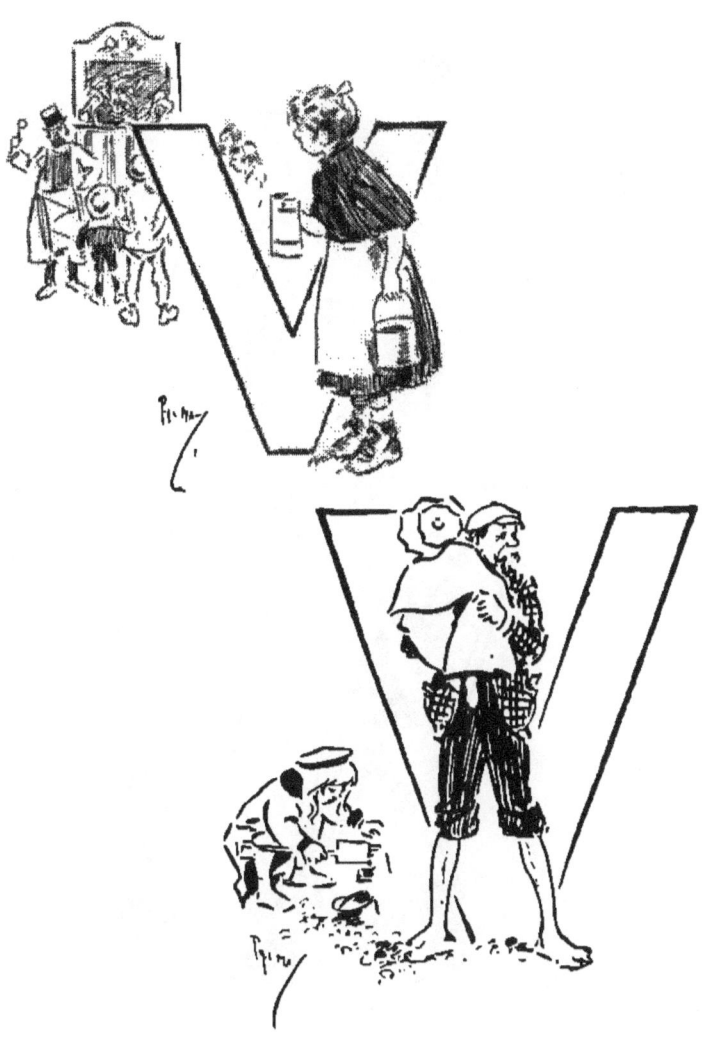

PHIL MAY'S
GUTTER-SNIPES

50
ORIGINAL SKETCHES
IN PEN & INK.

www.ingramcontent.com/pod-product-compliance
Lightning Source LLC
Chambersburg PA
CBHW022155020726
47496CB00008B/2720